Love Stories 2
A Collection of 8

BY

PATRICIA ANN PATH

Copyright © 2014 Patricia Path

All rights reserved.

ISBN:
ISBN-13:

DEDICATION

To my dear son, Rick, who recently passed away.
I miss him very much.

CONTENTS

	Acknowledgments	i
1	INNOCENT LOVE	1
2	TIL DEATH DO US PART	7
3	FLIGHT	11
4	THE HOUSE NEXT DOOR	15
5	BROKEN WINDOWS	20
6	VENGEANCE	24
7	AN ECHO OF LOVE	28
8	AND THEN THERE WAS HELL	32

ACKNOWLEDGMENTS

I am deeply grateful to
my son, Dan Acre,
my "adopted son" Kevin McGovern,
and my daughter, Gail Reynolds,
for their invaluable assistance in editing and compiling this book.

INNOCENT LOVE

It was a sunny fall day in Middleville, Indiana, as Loretta Nelson started out for school. "I'm leaving now, mother," she called as she left the house. "I'll see you later."

"Okay, dear," Pamela Nelson answered from the kitchen, where she was putting a roast in a crock pot for supper that night.

Loretta, a happy thirteen-year-old full of enthusiasm for life, was excited to be going into junior high school. It seemed as though she had been waiting all her life to finally be in the eighth grade. "I'm all grown up now," she said to herself on the way to school.

The school building was only blocks away from her home. It sat on a side street just below the "big hill" that all the kids loved to slide down in the winter time. Beyond the hill, a trail led into a wooded area, which sloped gradually downward to a lake.

As Loretta entered the school, Eloise, her best friend, stood waiting for her.

"Loretta, guess what?" said Eloise. "There's a new boy in our class. He's just scrumptious. I saved a seat for you right next to him; he would be just perfect for you, Loretta. If I didn't have Bryan, I'd sure go for him myself. Go for it, girl! Just a minute—your hair is mussed up again. I really think you need to get a perm. . . !"

The first bell interrupted Eloise's excitement, and the two girls hurried up the stairs to their home room.

As Loretta entered the classroom, she spotted the new boy right away, and fell in love with him at first sight. Oh, he's good looking, she thought happily as she slid into her seat next to him. Eloise was right. He's scrumptious.

He had dark, curly hair, Loretta noticed, and a few sprinkled freckles on his otherwise unblemished face. His arms were slightly tanned, in contrast to his light complexion. "This is going to be an interesting year," Loretta said almost out loud, observing the new boy flirtatiously. He smiled at her, but said nothing in response.

"You're late," the male teacher said to Loretta. "See that it doesn't happen again." Loretta responded affirmatively, pushing back strands of beautiful blond hair that had fallen a bit across her face.

The teacher continued, "Everyone, we have a new student this year. His name is Gerald Hurst. Jerry just moved here from Kansas City, Missouri. Please make him welcome."

Now I know his name, Loretta thought happily.

At lunch time, Eloise and Loretta sat across from Jerry in the cafeteria. As he sat eating quietly, Eloise, always the bolder of the two girls, introduced herself, then said, "This is my friend, Loretta. We're having a softball game out back after school today – girls against the boys to get acquainted with each other. Would you like to join us?" Jerry gave a big grin, and said, "Sure, I'll be there."

The ice broken, the three of them continued to chat through lunch. The girls learned that Jerry was staying with his grandmother temporarily until his family found a permanent house in town. They had wanted him to be able to start school on time, so had sent him on ahead while they closed down their bakery back home. They planned to open another bakery here in Middleville.

"That went well, don't you think?" Eloise said to Loretta as the two headed back to class.

After the game that day, Jerry approached Loretta after she had just said goodbye to Eloise. "Loretta, hold up," he said. "May I walk you home? I like you. You're a nifty first-base-man, and I'd like to get to first base with you."

Loretta's heart skipped a beat as she said jokingly, "Never! I'm waiting for my prince to come. You can walk me home, though. I'd like that, Jerry."

Jerry walked alongside her, glad to be with her, getting up the nerve to take her hand in his. Loretta welcomed the loving gesture, and the two walked along hand in hand, laughing and joking together. After they said goodbye at her house, Loretta burst in the door, calling out, "Mother, mother! I met a new boy at school today. He walked me home. I'm in love mother! I'm in love!"

"That's nice," Loretta's mother answered, absorbed in a mystery novel and not really listening.

One day when they were together, Jerry said to Loretta, "I've never been over that hill behind the school yet. Would you like to go see what's on the other side of it?"

"Sure," said Loretta.

They went up over the hill, and the very first day, they found their spot. It was under a big oak tree at the very edge of the wooded area. "This is wonderful, Loretta," said Jerry. "Who would ever dream of a lake and woods being hidden here over this hill? This oak tree. . .let's make this our spot."

Loretta agreed, "Yes, this will be our spot." And she looked into his eyes, pleading for him to kiss her. He took her in his arms, and gave Loretta her very first kiss—-and his.

A flock of geese flew over, honking, breaking the spell.

Jerry and Loretta came back down to earth, and sat quietly under the tree, welcoming the unfamiliar and disturbing feelings that were coming to life inside their bodies. "I've got to take you home," Jerry finally said. "You're my girl from now on. Okay?" Loretta, still mesmerized by the moment, nodded yes, and together they made their way down the hill.

My first kiss, Loretta happily thought.

Eventually the two arrived back at Loretta's house. "We'll take a lunch next time, Jerry," Loretta said.

"How about tomorrow?" Jerry said.

Loretta agreed. "Until tomorrow," she said, and he left her at her doorstep.

And so it went. Every day, the two went with their picnic lunch to their spot under the big oak tree on the edge of the woods. They kissed, and their kisses became more and more ardent. . .until that fateful day when they went too far.

Afterwards, Loretta started crying. Jerry tried to comfort her, but she said, "Get away from me, Jerry. Now look what you've done. You've ruined everything!"

Loretta abruptly got up and ran down the hill, leaving Jerry speechless. He ran after her. He called out her name, but she ignored him, and ran to her home.

For days, Jerry went back to Loretta's home and asked for her, but day after day, she refused to see him. At school she wouldn't speak to him or look his way.

He was heartbroken.

But Loretta was guilt-ridden about what she had done; so much so that her parents sent her away to a private school in another town. "I guess that's that," Jerry said, as he saw her one last time, getting into the family car with a suitcase, to leave his life forever.

Life went on. Jerry graduated from high school. Having decided to become a doctor, he entered medical school. He had continued to ask around about Loretta, but no one seemed to know anything about her except that she wasn't coming back to Middleville. No one knew where she was except her family.

"Someday," he would say to himself. For he never gave up hope of seeing Loretta again. He loved her. There was no other woman in his life. He lived with the memories of his and Loretta's friendship, hoping that someday they would be together again.

One day, as Jerry was walking along the path on their hill (after thinking, under the oak tree), he decided, I'll join the Peace Corps, to forget the pain I feel at losing Loretta's love.

And, after doing just that, he was sent to a remote African village to be a doctor at an orphanage that was run by the Catholic Church. The sisters there made him comfortable, in a makeshift shelter next to the orphanage. Let God heal me, he thought.

One day, the sisters were busy preparing the children for the doctor to examine them. One sister called out to another who was standing off by herself a bit: "Sister Loretta, don't be shy. I want you to meet Doctor Hurst; you'll be working with him regularly. Hurry, he needs your help with the children!"

Jerry looked at the approaching sister, and realized, in amazement. . .It's Loretta!

Their eyes met. Loretta gave a gasp, and then said with a slightly unsteady voice, "Welcome, Doctor Hurst. I will be your nurse in attendance."

With his heart jumping, Jerry calmly answered, "Thank you, Sister Loretta. I think we'll do fine together. Hand me a bandage, please. This child has a laceration over her eye; we don't want it to get infected." It was a wonderful act. Inside, his heart was pounding, and he had broken out in a cold sweat.

Loretta wasn't faring much better. She managed to gently say, "Yes, doctor," trembling as she handed him the bandage.

The day passed. And that night, Jerry became aware of someone at the doorway of his dwelling. He turned and looked.

It was Loretta.

They fell into each other's arms, and their bodies awakened to a need rekindled from all the years apart.

They gently but urgently became one. And afterwards, Loretta whispered to Jerry, "My prince has come." They were married not long after, by a priest. Loretta had left the sisterhood. But she and Jerry stayed on to take care of the children's medical needs. And the children called Loretta "Princess," for that was the name the doctor gave her.

TIL DEATH DO US PART

Alicia had just left Tyler, the love of her life, to go home to her ailing husband. On the way home, in her beat-up old Ford, she remembered her parting words with Tyler.

"Tyler," she said," my husband was just diagnosed with cancer. I can't follow through with the divorce and marry you now, Dear Heart. I wouldn't be able to live with myself."

Tyler pleaded with her. "But Alicia, I love you. You are my life. I want and need you."

"He's sick, Tyler. I can't leave him now," she responded.

"Of, course you can't. I was only thinking of us. Your devotion to your husband should not waver at this time of crisis for him. If we must break up, that is what it will be. I love you, Alicia, and always will. How long does he have?" Tyler asked sympathetically.

"I don't know ... maybe he can beat it. We're hoping and praying for a miracle, love of my life. But I must do what I have to do.

Goodbye forever."

Alicia's mind came back to the present. She wiped the tears from her eyes and blew her nose before walking bravely to her door after parking her car in their driveway.

David met her at the door. "Lishie, did you get my prescription filled?" he asked, weakly.

"Yes," she answered. "Lay down and rest, dear. I'll get it ready for you. Give me a minute."

"Thank you, sweets. What would I ever do without you? Those treatments make me so sick."

"I know, dear," Alicia answered. "It will just be a minute. By the time you're settled down in bed, I'll have your medicine to you."

"Okay, Lishie, you're the boss," David answered.

David was in his third week of treatment, and was sick most of the time since starting. Alicia took care of him faithfully, day after day, with no end, it seemed, and no hope of him getting better. But slowly and surely he got better. Finally, the doctor gave David the okay. He had beaten cancer! Soon, David was back to work, and everything was back to normal.

Alicia had mixed feelings. She loved David, but her body yearned for Tyler's kisses. She missed the smell of Tyler's cologne and the way his face flushed when she gave him a compliment. It's too late now, she thought at quiet moments when she was alone. Tyler's lost and gone forever out of my life. I'll never see him again. Yes, she cared for her husband and was good to him, but Tyler had stolen her heart. She missed him body and soul. Alicia suffered silently, never telling anyone of her secret love for him.

The years went by, and try as she might, Alicia couldn't forget about

Tyler. She daydreamed about him every chance she got.

On their tenth anniversary, five years after Alicia had broken up with Tyler, she and David went out to a fancy restaurant to celebrate.

"Hurry Lishie," David said, "Not only are we celebrating our anniversary, but I also got a raise today at work. Now we can afford that vacation to Paris that I always wanted for you." David was happy.

They arrived at the "El Royale Restaurant" just as the sun was setting in the western sky. There was a large Happy Anniversary sign on the wall by their table inside the restaurant. David had thought of everything. The couple was in good spirits as they ordered their favorite dinner, Swiss Steak and Mushrooms. The wine was chilled to perfection, and they were at the height of their celebration when Alicia happened to glance at the table just ahead of them.

My God, Alicia thought. It's him, Tyler! He's with someone. Could it be he got married? Watching Tyler, Alicia remembered when it was she by Tyler's side, not someone else. Sadly and soberly, Alicia excused herself from the table and headed for the ladies room. She held back tears.

Alicia freshened her makeup at the mirror over the sink and, after steadying her nerves, started back to their table where her loyal husband waited. Outside the door of the ladies room, Tyler stood waiting. Their eyes held as they gave each other a long-forbidden look of lust and unfulfilled love. Alicia started to speak but turned away abruptly for fear their fleeting moment would be noticed. Tyler called after her, but she half-ran back to her table.

Seeing her drawn face, David said, "You look like you've seen a ghost. Are you alright?"

Alicia smiled weakly and said, "I just had a weak moment, David, dear. It was probably the drinks."

About that time, Tyler approached their table. Alicia's heart started beating heavily and her whole body shook.

Tyler spoke. "Miss," he said, "You dropped this." Alicia thanked him meekly, and Tyler was gone, back to his table to be with the beautiful brunette waiting for him.

It was a folded piece of paper that Tyler gave Alicia. She carefully opened it up and read:

"Meet me at 7:00 P.M. Wednesday at our old Haunt."

Alicia quickly crumpled up the note and put it in her purse. "Cheer up, Alicia," David said, just at that moment. "Let's have a toast, my dear wife of 10 years." He held up his glass. "Until death do us part," he said. With mixed feelings, Alicia touched her glass to his, her heart beating wildly in anticipation of Wednesday at 7:00 PM, until her conscience kicked in telling her it was wrong and it would never be right. She realized her place was with her husband, and then she experienced a dull ache in her heart.

David cut her a piece of the anniversary cake as Alicia yearned for unfulfilled dreams of Tyler and yesterday. Just at that moment, she saw Tyler look back at her, his eyes begging her to be his as he left the restaurant with the lovely brunette at his side.

She wondered fearfully - Will I be strong enough to resist the temptation of meeting Tyler Wednesday? Sadly, Alicia accepted the piece of the 10th anniversary cake that her loyal husband had given to her.

FLIGHT

It was a hot and humid moonless night as a truck bearing the name "Lopez Freight" made its way down a lonely Mexican highway with its cargo of new refrigerators from a Mexican factory. The shipment was scheduled to arrive in the United States by Friday, two days away.

As the truck's motor purred steadily along the highway, voices were heard from within, amongst the cargo.

A little six-year-old boy, huddled with his mother inside an empty refrigerator box in the back of the truck, said, "I want to go home, Mother. It's hot in here--I can hardly breathe. I want to be with my friends."

His mother, reaching out for him, pulling him into her arms to comfort him, answered, "Hush, Manuel. We must be quiet. If they hear us, they will send us to prison, or worse. Your father is waiting for us in America. Be patient. We, too, will soon be in America with your father. He has a good job, Manuel, as a gardener for a rich man. Your father says that I will be hired as a maid for this man. The man promised him. We will then have money to buy you a pair of shoes, Manuel. Wouldn't you like a new pair of shoes?"

"I have shoes," Manuel sorrowfully explained to his mother, Maria. "I just forgot to bring them. We hurried so to get to the truck before it left without us. Besides, I don't like Jake, the driver. He's mean. He swore at me."

"Never mind, Manuel," Maria said, comforting her son. "We'll soon be with your father to start a new life in America."

"Yes, mama," Manuel said, wiping the sweat from his brow.

"Come, Manuel," Maria said, encouragingly, "while the truck is moving, let's get out of this box and stretch our legs. We will be cooler outside this refrigerator box. They crawled out of their hiding place. "Isn't this better?" she asked hopefully.

"I have to go to the bathroom, Mama," Manuel complained.

Patiently, Maria answered, "Go in the corner in the tin bucket hidden there. Here, take the flashlight. Be careful, little one."

The boy took the flashlight from his mother's loving hands and did as she said.

As Maria and Manuel slept, the truck rolled on. It finally arrived at a border checkpoint, bringing mother and child that much closer to freedom.

At the checkpoint, the border agent checked the truck driver's license. "Are you Jake Jenkins?" he asked.

After a pause, the driver answered, "Yes."

"I'm sorry, Mr. Jenkins, we have a warrant out for your arrest for violating probation," were the agent's ominous words.

As Jake was taken away, the truck was driven to a remote holding area, out of earshot of the border agents—forgotten by all for the present time. Inside, Maria and Manuel, awakened, huddled in fear of discovery. The border agent had left them there, not knowing that there were stowaways on the truck.

Time passed. Marie, now fearful, realized that they had been abandoned, with no hope of ever seeing her husband again. She cried quietly, sadly aware of her fate.

Daylight came, and as the day passed, the inside of the abandoned truck grew stifling from the hot sun shining down. It became hard to breathe for Maria and Manuel. Panicking now, they started screaming, and pounding on the truck's doors. They were trapped! The two ate their meager supply of cornmeal mush sparingly, and took little sips from a jug of tepid water to quench their thirst. They prayed that someone would hear their cries for help and free them from their prison.

Days passed. No one came.

With their water and food supply gone, and their throats hoarse from screaming for help, Maria and Manuel died silently, huddled together for comfort in each other's arms, inside the forgotten and seemingly abandoned truck. "Someone will come soon, Manuel," were Maria's last words as she clutched desperately to her dead son's body.

Week after week passed by. Nobody came.

Meanwhile, each day, at the agreed-upon time, Maria's husband, Juan, went to the agreed-upon meeting place where the truck was supposed to bring his precious family to him.

The truck never came.

Weeks later, the bodies were finally discovered by Jake, when, after beating the rap and being set free, he went to retrieve his truck. Fearing discovery, he buried the bodies by a clump of trees at the side of a lonely country road, and then finished his task of delivering the refrigerators to their destination.

One day, Juan received the news from the man for whom he worked that his family was no longer alive. Juan cried. The rich man cried. Manuel and Maria could no longer cry. They were gone from the Earth forever.

THE HOUSE NEXT DOOR

It was a peaceful Sunday afternoon finding Holly Jacobs alone at the kitchen table waiting patiently for the back door to open. Her husband, Marvin, was next door at their neighbor's home, mowing the grass. Their neighbor, Alice Connors, had just recently lost her husband. She was now a widow. Holly and Marvin had taken it upon themselves to look out for her.

Alice, a young woman of 22 years, a little younger than Holly, seemed so helpless at the present time. "Marvin," Holly had said to her husband just today, "she seems so lost. When I went to visit her she spoke few words and just sat staring at her husband Benjamin's picture. Go over there and cheer her up, dear. I don't know what to say to her."

"Well, neither do I, Holly. I can't bring her husband back. What can I do about it?" Marvin argued.

"Well, Marvin, do something! Cut her grass for her and take out her trash. She hasn't been outside since the funeral. You know she's got trash that needs throwing out by now," Holly had answered.

That was three hours ago.

"I didn't plan on Marvin staying this long," a worried Holly complained restlessly. "What could be keeping him? Marvin finished mowing the lawn an hour ago."

There were footsteps on the back porch. In walked Marvin.

"What took you so long, Marvin? You've been gone 3 hours. There's liquor on your breath, too! You never drink!"

Marvin sat down across from her. "She asked if I would have a couple of drinks with her, Holly. She's a mess. She must have been drinking since early."

"Great! If I knew you were going to stay so long, I wouldn't have asked you to go see about her. And drinking too. What on earth?" Holly said with disgust.

"Alice had a bad childhood," said Marvin sympathetically.

"Great! Now she's told you her life story. This isn't working out at all like I thought it would," Holly exclaimed.

"Now, honey, she's a widow. She's just lost her husband. We've got to do what we can," said Marvin.

Holly frowned. "That's not what you thought a few hours ago. Oh, what liquor will do!"

Marvin hiccuped. "I do believe you're jealous! Oh, come on. You can trust me. She just needs someone during this rough spell." Marvin went to the living room to watch television.

As time went on, things got worse between Holly and Marvin. There were phone calls from Alice. "Holly dear, may I borrow your husband? My sink is stopped up," or "my washer needs fixing again. And Marvin does such a good job keeping it working for me!"

Holly would sweetly tell Alice, "I'll see if he's available."

Marvin was always available - in more ways than one, it seemed to Holly. But she had no way of stopping it.

"You're just jealous," Marvin would say each time she complained. "You're worrying your little head over nothing. Trust me, I'm your husband. But we can't let Alice down. She has no one."

Then it all was brought out into the open. Alice became pregnant with Marvin's baby!

Marvin, caught now in his own game, said, "It is what it is, Holly. She has no one. That doesn't mean I love you any less. Don't divorce me, honey. I love you, but Alice needs us. We can't let her down."

Holly was miserable, but she told herself, "My husband loves us both. I can't let her win. Marvin is mine. He doesn't want a divorce. I'll just have to live with it that Marvin has a child by another woman."

All Holly's friends suspected the obvious, but Holly hung on for dear life. "What am I going to do?" she asked herself. She endlessly searched her soul for answers. Then one day the answer came to her. "I know," she said aloud. "I'll find a mate for Alice. That's the only way." Holly got started on it right away.

It wasn't long until she found someone.

It was the day that Holly's best friend, Faye, called excitedly. "Holly," she said, "My husband's brother is coming to live with us for awhile. He would be ideal for Alice. Should I throw a party and invite her?"

Holly was ecstatic. "Wonderful news, Faye. By all means, throw a party. I've got to get this spider out of my parlor. That's what Alice is

– a treacherous spider, spinning her web to trap my husband! I'd never survive without my husband."

"Just hang in there," said Faye. "The fix-it-all party is coming up!"

"If you can pull that off, I'll owe you for the rest of my days," Holly said with gratitude. The two then hung up, planning for their answer to Holly's problem.

It was a great party, and it worked. Alice and Neil Smith, Faye's brother-in-law, hit it off well together. They became a couple. At first, Marvin pouted and moped about the house, but Holly, being a wise wife, wooed him back into her love nest. The plan seemed perfect until 3 years later, when the phone rang. It was Alice. "Holly," she said, "let me talk to Marvin. It's very important!"

Holly called Marvin to the phone.

"Hello, Marvin. This is Alice. Our son, Tommie, is dead! He ran in front of a car while going over to my friend Sharon's house. I need you, Marvin! What am I going to do? My little boy, our son, Marvin. Come quick. I'm at the hospital. The police are here. Hurry Marvin, hurry!"

Marvin's face turned white and he started shaking as he said to Holly, "Tommie is dead. Our son is dead. He ran in front of a car."

Holly stared in disbelief. "Go, Marvin. You must."

A few minutes later there was a knock at the door. It was Neil, still single, for he and Alice had never married. "Holly," Neil greeted her when the door opened, "I thought you might need me. Alice didn't."

And he was right, need him she did, for Marvin spent long hours, day after day, with Alice, consoling her. Then one day, Marvin moved next door, lock, stock, and barrel, to live with Alice. "You can do what you must, Holly, for Alice needs me. And I love her," were his parting words.

Holly had no choice. She had lost him. She got a divorce, but by this time it didn't matter, for Neil had been there for her through it all. They fell in love, and soon after the divorce, Neil asked her to marry him. Holly said yes.

On the day of their marriage, Alice and Marvin looked over their fence at Holly and Neil's backyard reception. A wise old owl knew what they were thinking. They knew that the love they had been craving had suddenly slipped from their fingers to the couple laughing happily together in the backyard of the house next door. Marvin and Alice were left empty.

BROKEN WINDOWS

It was a rainy, overcast day as Bryan Henderson and his mother, Paula Henderson, traveled down a Michigan highway. Bryan's mother was a widow, and she had no other family member that she could depend on for comfort in her and Bryan's lonely existence. Mother and son forged onward through the many obstacles that life had dealt them. In spite of rough times, they were happy together.

Today was a special day. It was Bryan's 7th birthday, and they were on their way home from visiting John Ball Park in Grand Rapids. Traffic was heavy as they drove along to their humble home on the edge of a little town many miles north of Grand Rapids.

"Did you have a good time at John Ball Park, Bryan?" Paula asked her son.

"Yes, Mother," he said between yawns, for now he was tired and sleepy after such an exciting day.

"It looks like you could use a nap. Why don't you lay your head back and rest? It will be a while before we're home." Paula loved her son with all her heart. It wasn't long before Bryan nodded off to sleep, and all was quiet except for the steady hum of the car engine.

Then it happened. A deer stepped into the road in front of them, and Paula veered to avoid hitting it. The car skidded off the road, out of control. It overturned into a gully, where it rolled over and over. There was no time to even scream. Paula could only wrap her arms around Bryan to protect him from the full impact. There was shattering of metal and glass, and the car rolled until it suddenly hit a tree broadside and stopped. Then there was silence.

Soon someone arrived at this horrendous scene. An ambulance came soon after. It was too late for the bleeding Paula. She was dead. But Bryan, covered with blood, cried out "Mother! Mother! Wake up, Mother!" But it was in vain. Paula had left this earth, never to see her only loved one, her son, ever again.

Bryan refused to leave the side of his mother's dead body, and clutched desperately to the only loved one he had. But they pulled him away and put him in the ambulance. Sirens blared as they were transported to the nearest hospital. Tears moistened the ambulance driver's mind as his mind went back to the cross that hung from the broken rear view mirror of the Henderson's car. "Why, God? Why?" he asked aloud in sadness.

Bryan recovered from his injuries quickly and was released from the hospital two days later. He was placed in a foster home not far from where he and his mother had once resided. Mrs. Erickson, his foster mother, treated Bryan kindly, and her husband occasionally took him fishing. But nothing would erase the sadness that Bryan was feeling. He was very unhappy and sometimes rebellious towards Mrs. Erickson, shouting, "You're not my mother!" before going to his room in tears.

Then one day Bryan came up missing. The neighborhood was searched, to no avail. Finally, the police were notified, and on the lookout for a 7-year-old brown haired, freckle-faced boy last seen in a red T-shirt and blue jeans.

The police decided to look for Bryan at his former residence on Myrtle Street, two miles away from his foster home. Officer Smith of the Police Department found him crying on the sidewalk in front of the abandoned home. He approached the child slowly and carefully in order not to frighten him. "Hello, Bryan," he said, "Mrs. Erickson is worried about you. Let's take you back to her. There's nothing you can do here, son."

Bryan started sobbing all the harder.

"Here, now, Bryan, it can't be that bad. You've got to go back to Mr. and Mrs. Erickson," said Officer Smith.

Bryan refused to budge. "No. This is my home, officer, and the front windows are broken out. Someone threw rocks at the home that my mother and I lived in. I can't leave. I've got to guard my mother's home. They took me away from my mother and told me she was dead. My mother isn't dead. I want my mother. Mother will be back. I've got to wait for her. She's just sick. She'll get better."

Officer Smith, shaken and saddened by this little boy's plight, bent down beside him. "I'll tell you what, Bryan. Let's fix those broken windows. Let's go to the hardware store and get someone to fix them right now. I'll guard your home from now on."

The cop and the small boy went to Atkinson's Hardware Store, and one of the clerks grabbed some tools and a ladder. They went to Bryan's abandoned home, and in no time, after cutting some new glass, the windows were repaired. Bryan and Officer Smith stood by, watching.

Bryan, with a smile on his face, took Officer Smith's hand and agreed to go back to the foster home.

Officer Smith took him there. Before getting out of the police car, Bryan looked at Officer Smith and said, "Tell me if my mother is dead.

You wouldn't lie to me. You are a policeman."

Officer Smith cleared his throat, and with his voice shaking, moved by the moment, answered the trusting child. "Yes, Bryan, your mother has passed on and left this earth, but I believe she is now in heaven with your father. They're both watching over you from heaven. Your mother and father loved you very much and they still do."

Bryan, his bottom lip trembling, straightened up his shoulders and said, "My mother is in heaven with my dad. I will miss her. Will you come and visit me, Officer Smith?"

And that is how a young police officer and a sad, lost little boy found each other. Officer Smith was so moved by this little boy's lot in life that he and his childless wife bought Bryan's former home, and they adopted Bryan as their very own son. They now all live happily together at 918 Myrtle Avenue, the formerly abandoned home that Bryan loved.

VENGEANCE

In a small Eastern town on a street named Tranquil Lane, there lived a married couple, Darrel and Carlotta Smithens. They lived comfortably in a beautiful brick home and were envied by everyone for their seemingly perfect marriage. Darrel, a hard-working executive at a pharmaceutical company, was highly respected in the community, as was his loving wife, known to be a very pious woman who attended church regularly and gave of herself to help those in need. "A perfect marriage," their friends and neighbors often said of them.

But today, a Tuesday in late March, Carlotta was very upset and unhappy.

While straightening up their bedroom, she bent down to pick up Darrel's suit jacket, which had slipped from the back of a chair and landed in a heap on the floor. As she picked up the jacket, a folded piece of paper fell out of its pocket. "What's this?" she wondered aloud, and picked up the note and opened it. As she read, her heart began to beat wildly in fear:

"Darling Darrel, Are we still on for tomorrow night? We belong together, my darling. My body yearns for your hugs and kisses. Can we go to the Beach Side Motel again, like we did last time? I know that foolish religious fanatic of a wife trusts you, but what are you going to tell her this time? I think we're both running out of excuses. Let's just run away together. Love, Trixie."

Carlotta, sat in an easy chair in the living room, and cried silently, not wanting to believe what she had just read. "Darrel is unfaithful to me," she wailed. "Now what do I do?" Seeking comfort, she picked up her Bible and read a few pages, none of it registering on her. She was in shock. Her body numb, she got up slowly, and determinedly made her way to the bedroom. Once there, she opened the top dresser drawer, and withdrew from its secret place there, a pistol.

"And now, the bullets," she said, finding these as well, and loading them into the pistol. Her face ashen, she then said in a near-whisper, "Lord, I'm going to kill Darrel. He's been cheating on me, Lord. He must die."

As if in a trance, she went back to the living room, and sat back in the easy chair, placing the pistol on an end table to the side.

She picked up the Bible again, and began to read, coldly and distantly.

The day passed slowly. Carlotta held the Bible in her lap, read a page now and again, often staring at the front door unforgivingly, waiting for her husband to come home. "He is doing me wrong," she said repeatedly, without tears, agitatedly rocking her body to and fro.

Their grandfather clock chimed out every hour. She counted them with anticipation. Soon it will be time, she would think, not blinking, staring coldly at the door.

"He will be here soon, Lord," she said at one point.

Later, growing impatient, she said, "How much longer, Lord?"

Not long after that, she mused, "I don't want to live. I'll kill myself instead of him. Is that what I should do, Lord?" And she put the gun to her head. But, changing her mind, she said, "No, Lord, I'm already dead inside. My husband is wronging me. He's the one who deserves to die." And she lowered the gun.

The day dragged on. Carlotta left the chair only occasionally, to go to the bathroom or get a drink of water. Once, she decided to water her plants, and so lovingly, with great care.

Finally, midnight arrived, as the clock chimed twelve times. "How much longer must I wait, Lord?" she said. "How much longer?" Her body trembled as she contemplated what she was about to do. "I must kill him," she whispered. "There is no other answer. An eye for an eye and a tooth for a tooth."

Then. . .at about 1:00 am. . .she heard the lock turn in the door. "He's home," she whispered hoarsely.

She quickly picked up the gun and hid it under a pillow on her lap; the Bible fell to the floor, landing by her feet, the pages fluttering open.

Darrel walked in the door, and saw his wife sitting in the chair. "You're still up, Carlotta?" he asked. "How come?"

"I read the note from Trixie, Darrel. How could you do that to me? I hate you," she said, and pulled the gun out from under the pillow and pointed it at him. "I'm going to kill you, Darrel. Do you have anything to say before you die?"

"Carlotta, listen to me," Darrel said in sudden desperation. "Trixie and I broke up tonight. We had a big fight; it's over. She was nothing to me. You're the one I love. I made a mistake; I'm sorry! For God's sake, Carlotta, put the gun down!"

Carlotta's eyes narrowed, as she steadied herself, preparing to pull the trigger, but hesitating a moment.

"No! Carlotta! Don't do it!" he pleaded. "I'll never be unfaithful again!"

Suddenly the front door flew open. It was Trixie, enraged, a gun in her hand. "Die, you ungrateful scum!" she shouted, pointing the gun at Darrel and firing before he could react. He fell to the floor, dead. Trixie observed him a moment, realizing what she had done, and then screamed hysterically. She put the gun to her head—-and fired again. She fell to the floor, near Darrel. . .lifeless as well.

Carlotta observed the two bodies on the floor for some moments. Then she rose, went to the phone, and carefully dialed 9-1-1. She reported a murder-suicide to the dispatcher, one that she had witnessed. She hung up, and walked to where her Bible had fallen to the floor. Opening it somewhat casually, her eyes fell on the underlined passage of Romans 12:19. She read in awe. "Vengeance is mine, I will repay, saith the Lord."

Carlotta smiled.

AN ECHO OF LOVE

Martha, a single mother with one daughter named Daisy, was home sick from work today. Daisy had not yet gotten home from school when Martha went to retrieve her daily newspaper, which had landed on her porch with a thump.

Martha sat down in her easy chair and proceeded to turn the paper, as she always did, to the obituaries.

Ever since her mother had passed away, she made it a habit to read each one to see if she knew any of those who had passed on.

This day, the obituaries had this:

John Samuels, local business man, husband of Naomi and father of only child, Brenda, left to be with our everlasting father this day, Wednesday, August 5th, 2010.

Martha's face turned white and her grief spilled over as she uttered the words, "John, my one and only love, father of my child. My John. It's been 9 years to the day since we broke up, just before Daisy was born. He was going to get a divorce. Why him, God? Why him? Daisy must never know he was her father, and I won't tell her now."

She sobbed as she continued. "I told her her father was a stunt pilot and got killed while flying a plane, and that's all she needed to know. I then told her never to ask me again."

Continuing, she said, "I can't tell her the truth - that he was married and had his own family."

About that time Daisy came bursting into the house. "Mama, Mama," she said, "I've got something to tell you. One of my friends from Girl Scouts' father died. She came to Scouts today. She felt she had to be there, for she had something to ask me. She wants me to come to the funeral home tonight and be with her. I'm her best friend, mother, we've just got to go."

Oh, no, could it be? Not my John, Martha thought to herself. "What is your friend at Scouts' name, Daisy?" she asked.

"Her name is Brenda, mother. I can't let Brenda down. We can bring a bouquet of roses from your garden. I know how hard for you to make ends meet. She is sad, Mother, so sad," said Daisy, remembering.

Martha said a silent prayer. "What should I do, Lord? Help me through this."

Drawing strength from within her very being she said, "By all means, Daisy, we'll be there at 7:00 p.m. so you can be with your friend."

Daisy gave her mother a swift hug and said, "Thank you, Mother, I love you."

When Martha and Daisy entered Scott's Funeral Home, where her friend's father laid to rest, the haunting smell of flowers was prevalent. Dreading every step of the way, Martha, with Daisy, entered the room where John's casket was located. Brenda sadly greeted Daisy, hugging her tightly, while giving Martha a brief, tear-stained smile.

Martha thought sadly to herself: "To think I never knew that Daisy was friends with My John's daughter Brenda, with Daisy not knowing that she, Daisy, was also John's daughter. Does his wife realize the connection? No, she didn't know that John and I were lovers. I doubt if anyone knew of our relationship. It was a very discreet affair. We were never able to tell the world of our love for each other. Oh, God, my one and only love gone from the earth forever and I'm not allowed to show my grief for fear of exposure. Here comes his wife, I think. I'm not sure. God, now what do I do?"

The grief-stricken widow walked over to Martha accusingly. "You're Martha, aren't you? I found your picture with the telling signature of "I'm yours forever. Martha." All these years--I've been blind to you until I found your picture hidden in his wallet yesterday. All those lonely nights I spent when he lied to me and told me he had to go out of town on business. That business was you, wasn't it? Is Daisy his child? The resemblance? Please don't let it be."

"I'm sorry, Mrs. Samuels. Yes, Daisy is his child, but she doesn't know your husband is her father. We loved each other, Mrs. Samuels. I'm sorry," Martha sorrowfully said.

"You don't belong here. Take your daughter and go. I will not permit Brenda and her to be friends anymore. I hate you. Be gone. Go! Get out!" Mrs. Samuels whispered hoarsely, just loud enough for only Martha to hear.

Martha and Daisy left abruptly.

Brenda watched as her mother, Mrs. Samuels, went to her husband's casket, threw her rings at him, screaming "I hate you, you bastard. May your soul rot in hell!" She then told the funeral director to close the casket saying, "Close this casket. This man is no longer my husband. Bury him as soon as possible. There will be no more visitation."

She called to Brenda and said, "We're going home. Don't mention your father's name to me ever again!"

"Why mother? Why?" Brenda was sobbing to her mother as mother and child left the room of their dead loved one.

On the way home, Martha held in her sadness, being brave for her only daughter. Daisy said, "I'm glad I never knew my pilot father, mother, for I would have been so sad at his death."

Martha could no longer hold back the tears. Through her sobs she said, "Yes, Daisy, I'll miss him forever, but I have you to remember him by. You are my echo of love."

AND THEN THERE WAS HELL

Clare Jean, a young mother of 4 children, and separated from her husband, Leon, had just received an unwelcome phone call while sitting in the kitchen observing a cockroach on the wall.

After hanging up the phone, she picked up her cup of coffee. Sipping from the cup, she looked around the kitchen. One of the kids had left jelly smeared across the counter. A couple of roaches were having a sweet feast there. She'd have to clean that up.

The kids were all asleep, and she was feeling jittery. The big house felt sad and empty when the kids were asleep. In tears, she uttered a sad, woe-begotten sigh. She picked up the phone and dialed her old friend Martha, who had just moved back into town after living in Florida for ten years. They had a lot of catching up to do, since they hadn't spoken to each other in all that time. She twisted the phone cord between her fingers as she waited for Martha to answer. The only light in the house was here in the kitchen.

"Martha? It's Clare Jean. Yes! I was so surprised to see you at the store. Ten years! And you still look so pretty!" Clare Jean shifted on the stool, the phone receiver at her ear. She looked around for her cigarettes. They were under the stool. "I've got four kids now," she said. "Tell me, what was it like living in Florida."

Clare Jean listened silently while reaching down to pick up her cigarettes off the floor. She pulled one from the pack and lit it. As smoke trailed from her mouth, she brought the rim of coffee cup to her lips. Just as she was about to sip, she saw a cockroach perched on the opposite rim of the cup.

"My God!" Clare Jean dropped the phone receiver on the floor and quickly stood. The coffee cup tumbled onto the dirty tiles, splashing coffee across the floor. Clare Jean shivered in disgust as the cockroach crawled from the puddle of coffee and ran under the refrigerator, leaving a shiny, wet trail.

Oh, Lord!

Clare Jean slowly picked up the receiver and, after examining it closely, put it to her ear.

'I'm sorry, Martha. It was, it was," and then suddenly Clare Jean's shame and embarrassment, her sadness and fear, her disappointment, her precarious situation, all came pouring out through tears. She sat again on the stool.

"My God, Martha, what am I going to do? My mother from across state just called. She says she'll be here tomorrow to visit for a few days. There's no way I can hide these filthy cockroaches. They're everywhere! What will mom say? I'm so ashamed. And I'm so broke that there's no money for an exterminator. Yesterday, the kids had to help me search the couch cushions for money for a pack of cigarettes."

Clare Jean's too-thin body shook between sobs at the thought of her mother arriving and seeing the cockroaches. She lit another cigarette and continued to tell Martha of her woes.

"I haven't seen mother in a year. I can't refuse her if she wants to visit. It wouldn't do any good. Mom would just say, 'I'm coming anyway. You would deny me seeing my lovely grandchildren? I don't think so'."

A noise came from one of the bedrooms. A child's dream-babbles. "Hold on, Martha." Clare Jean held the phone away from her ear and listened. The sounds came from Sam's bedroom. He was a fitful sleeper. After a moment, silence returned to the dim house.

"Sorry, Martha. One of the boys is having a dream. Have you got a few minutes? Great. Thank you. So my husband Leon and I were together in our cozy home we had only owned for 3 years when I found out that he was cheating on me. How could he? I know he had been staying away 2 or 3 days at a time without my knowing where he was, but I laid it on to his heavy drinking and partying with his friend, Rob."

Clare watched a pair of large cockroaches race each other across the counter and disappear into the half-open silverware drawer. She stretched a leg out and carefully closed the drawer with her slippered foot.

"And the money! I should have guessed there was another woman in his life by him being away from home so long, but being naive and in love, I believed him when he said, 'I lost the money in a poker game.' A few months ago, he comes stumbling home one evening after being gone for two days, out carousing. He hands me twelve dollars, and says, 'Here, Babe, here's what's left. Buy some groceries. The kids have got to eat. When Rob and I are out, time goes by fast.'

I told him, 'I called work, Leon. They said you were at work but not allowed to take any phone calls unless it was an emergency. I left a message each time for you to call me but you never did. Why don't you ever answer my phone calls, Leon?'

So he says, 'Don't bug me, Clare Jean. I'm home now and you've got grocery money. Rob is my friend. We have fun together. You can either accept things as they are or get a divorce. I'm willing.' He was angry about it, and then he said, 'Fix me something to eat. I'm hungry.' And then, just like Dr. Jekyll and Mr. Hyde, he straightens up his shoulders and says, 'I'm sorry honey. It won't happen again. Don't leave me, Babe. You know I love you. You're the mother of my children. Where are they?'

I told him, 'Your mother has them for a few hours, Leon. She promised to take them to McDonald's.'

So he yawns and says, 'I'm going to bed. I don't want to see my mother. I'm not ready for one of her lectures. Forget the meal, I'll grab something at work. Iron me a shirt. I've got to go in early tomorrow. I've got to go in at 2:30 p.m. Give me extra clothes to take to work. I'll shower there.'

Then, as he was heading to the bedroom to sleep it off, I asked him, 'Are you going to the bar again tonight, Leon?'

He turns around and looks at me. 'For sure, honey. I'll be home tonight. Late. There's a sack of dirty clothes out in the car. Get them and wash them up for me, Sweet. Some are Rob's. I've got to get them back to him.' Did you get that, Martha? He brought home Rob's clothes for me to wash, like I'm some washerwoman!

So after Leon went into to the bedroom, I went out to the car and got the sack of dirty clothes to be washed. I'm saying to myself, 'I hope there's no lipstick on this batch of clothes. It's hard to get out.' When I confronted him about the lipstick before, he said it was mine. I used to believe him, but then I got smart and matched the colors to my own lipstick. It wasn't mine. Who was he trying to fool? I was angry with Leon, but even angrier with myself for putting up with his lame excuses. But again, I was just thankful that he was home again, safe from harm. What's that, Martha? Yeah, sure. I'll hang on."

While waiting for Martha to return to the line, Clare Jean grabbed a stiff washrag from the sink, rinsed it out under the faucet, and bent to clean the mess of coffee from the floor. Just as she was finishing, Martha came back on. Clare Jean cradled the phone between her shoulder and ear, talking as she rinsed out the washrag.

"Hey, you're back. Yeah, I'm here. I just cleaned up the floor. Spilled my coffee because a cockroach was about to use it for a bathtub. Yes, it's that bad. Are you sure? I don't want to bore you with my sad story. Well, okay then. Where was I? Oh yeah - so I went out and got the bag of laundry. Of course, it's Leon's and his friend's clothes. I washed them. Yes, Martha, I know. I did it. What could I do? I told myself, 'I should get a divorce, but damn it, I love him. It's a nightmare!' I also wondered how I'd pay my bills that month, and feed the kids, with twelve measly dollars. So I said to myself, 'I have to go to work. That's my only out.' So I started looking for work the next day. Of course, I had to be home to get the kids off to school, and to feed them when they got home. Who's going to hire me when I have those kinds of hours? That's right. Nobody. So I ended up babysitting the neighbor, Fran's, kids, as if I didn't have my hands full with my own. But it was something."

Clare Jean crushed out another cigarette. She looked into the pack to see how many were left. Not enough.

"Do you smoke, Martha? Uh huh. Yes, I tried to quit, but you know how it gets. I'm almost out for tonight."

Clare Jean lit another one.

"So I asked my dad how to deal with Leon. He said, 'Leon will straighten out some day. Just tuck him into bed when he comes home.' My father meant well.

So one day Leon decided to move out. He said he was going to live with Rob for a few months. He promised to call every day, and to give me money every payday to help with the bills. I didn't fight it much because I sensed that my marriage was ending, so what was the point? After he left, I realized that I had no idea where Rob lived. It was like that for a few months, and then Leon shows up in the middle of the night around Christmastime. He's half drunk, loud, and carrying a bunch of gifts for the kids. He says, 'Honey, I'm home! Merry Christmas!' I asked him if he was going to stay. He says, 'Yes, dear wife. I'm home to stay.' I was happy, and the kids were happy to see their dad.

But the next day, when he was sober and getting ready for work, he drops it on me. Here's what he says:

'Clare Jean, brace yourself. I was living with another woman by the name of Louise. She is divorced with 2 kids. We were out of fuel oil for her space heater and I left yesterday to get her some to tide her over until her welfare check came in. I'd spent most of my money on presents for the kids so could only buy her enough to get by. I didn't do it, Clare Jean. I got drunk instead. Here's her address. Can you take her a 5-gallon can of fuel oil to her? She's got kids, honey, and they'll freeze. My God, I hate myself sometimes, honey. Help me out of my jam, kitten? I'm home for good. It will be better for us honey, I promise. Here. Put the gifts under the tree.'

Well, naturally, I was shocked and insulted. So I says: 'You actually expect me to go to this Louise's house who harbored my husband with fuel oil to help her, your kept woman?'

So he's putting on his shorts now. He says to me, 'She has kids, Clare Jean. Remember the children. Here, read this, honey.'

Then he hands me a note she left in his pocket. I have it here. Can you hold on just a minute while I get it, Martha? You have to hear it. Okay. Just one sec."

Clare Jean got up and went into her bedroom. The note lay at the bottom of one of her dresser drawers. A moment later, she came back out and took a seat on the stool again. She put the phone to her ear and unfolded the note.

"Here it is, Martha. Are you there? Okay. I'm going to read it to you. She wrote in red ink. Maybe it's blood? Ha ha. Here it is:

Dear lover of my dreams. Go home to your wife and family. Don't let her too be a victim of a broken marriage. Remember the love we had together and build on it with a lasting loving relationship with your wife and family.
She loves you.
Goodbye my heart.
Louise

What a surprise, huh? She told him to go back to me. So I thought she was no problem, that she was no longer a threat to me. I was actually kind of relieved and thankful.

So I told Leon, 'Alright, I'll go. She means me no ill will.' And so I brought her the heating oil. And I took him back."

Clare Jean lit another cigarette and sighed. She ran her hands through her unkempt brown hair and looked around the kitchen. She counted seven cockroaches in plain view. One sat stationary on the counter, its feelers waving about. One was at the crack where the ceiling joined the top of the cupboard. Another crawled over a knob on the stove. Yet another explored the crumbs scattered around the toaster. And the pair at the jelly smear on the counter had been joined by a third.

"Yes, I'm still here Martha. Just daydreaming a bit," said Clare Jean into the phone. "So we had some happy times. Leon was coming home, there was money, and I was feeling better about things. Leon drank still, but not like before. Then it started again. The long hours away from home and the lipstick on the shirts. Then I got a phone call a couple of nights ago.

'Is Leon there?' It was a woman. 'This is Sharon. I need to talk to him.'

I asked her if she was the other woman.

'If you want to put it that way,' she says, 'I guess I am. I need to talk to Leon. He has my car keys in his pocket and I've got to go to work.'

So I called Leon to the phone. Then he hurried into the bathroom for a quick shower and shave. As he was leaving, I told him, 'Drop her! Do you hear me? You have no right putting me through this again. I mean it, Leon, drop her!'

He tells me, 'No, Clare Jean, I won't. We're in love.'

I'm angry now. So I tell him, 'Damn you, Leon! I'm getting a divorce this time.'

Then he says, 'Yes, Clare Jean, you better do that. I want my freedom. Besides you are a rotten cook. You didn't know that did you? It's been a nightmare choking down your rotten half-done meals. And the way you've let yourself go. You're the picture of ugly. I do mean ugly. Sharon is beautiful. I want to marry her. Did you hear me? I no longer love you. Goodbye, you poor excuse for a woman that makes love like a frozen toad.'

How do you like that, Martha? How could he say such things? So I said, 'Damn you, Leon! You've got a responsibility to the kids and me. What are we supposed to do? Do you know we're losing our home for not keeping up on payments? Don't you understand?'

He had the nerve to say, 'You should have managed the money better! Is that all you care about is money? Well your money tree had dried up! I'm leaving.'

Then he was gone. After standing there in shock for a minute, I called my mother. I said, 'Mother, Leon wants a divorce. Will you loan me the money to get it?'

But my mother is smart. She says to me, 'If Leon wants a divorce, let him pay for it. You've got to keep going for the children. See a lawyer to arrange for support. I'll send you a little money to tide you over, but let him get the divorce.'

Though it was nice that she was sending me money, it isn't enough to save the house. And I'm pregnant! And now she calls earlier tonight to tell me she's going to be here tomorrow. I'm so embarrassed, Martha!"

A small child in pajamas shuffled into the kitchen, rubbing his eyes. Clare Jean's three-year old, Sam.

"Hold on Martha," said Clare Jean. Then, to the child, "Sam, you're up? Can't sleep?"

"I want a drink of water," said Sam.

Clare Jean stood. "Martha, I have to get off the phone. Sam's up and I need to get him back to sleep. Can we talk again soon? Okay? Good. Yes – when we're both free."

Clare hung up the phone and picked up Sam. "Let's get you some water and then back to bed. What do you say?" she said.

At 3:00 p.m. the next day, Clare Jean's mother arrived. She took one look around and said, "Clare Jean you've got yourself in a mess this time. I can't stay here to help you with these filthy bugs crawling all over. Call me a cab and I'll get a room. Here, take this check to get rid of the damn bugs. And pack up the kids and be ready by next Saturday. Your dad will be after you. I'm getting sick from the bugs, Clare Jean. Hurry! Call me a cab."

The cab came, and Clare Jean's mother left.

Nothing could be heard in the room except the heartbroken sobs of Clare Jean as she clutched her mother's check.

In time you could hear the voices of the children as they entered their home from school.

"We're moving in a week to go live with your grandparents, kids." Clare Jean announced.

"Okay, Mom," was their reply as they stared sadly at the hunched over body of their mother sobbing tears of despair. The children knew their only hope was in their mother, since their father had left.

"Good, mother," little Jenna, the 8-year-old, said. "No more bugs."

Clare Jean agreed as if a dark cloud had lifted. "No more bugs."

They moved. After some time had passed for Clare Jean and her family in their new home with their grandparents, Clare Jean gave birth to a beautiful baby boy. She named him Alexander Graham, for his birth brought a phone call from Leon wanting to start over fresh.

"Clare Jean, your folks called and told me to come get the older kids and take care of them. I'll be over to pick them up. I'm staying at my mother's now. It didn't work out with Sharon. I won't be up to see you or the baby. Are you sure the baby is mine?"

"Oh, for God's sake, Leon, grow up!" Clare Jean said. "I've been going through hell. Don't make it any worse for me."

Leon was quiet for a moment before he said, "And then there was hell." He hung up without another word.

When Alexander and mother came home from the hospital, the two oldest children, Sadie and Sam, were gone. Their father had picked them up the day before, and Clare Jean wasn't able to say goodbye to them. She again thought of Leon's words "and then there was hell," for she had lost control of the whole situation.

Clare Jean's mother demanded that Leon pay money each week to support the remaining 3 children left in her care. Of course they caused no trouble. They were good children.

One day Clare Jean's father called her into the kitchen saying, "Sit down, Clare Jean, and have a cup of coffee. It's time you and Leon went back together for the sake of the children. That is if you still love him. Do you?"

Clare Jean thought for a moment and said, "I don't hate him father, but if I love him, I'm not feeling it at the moment. I don't know. My furniture is in storage. I'd have to hunt a place to live. And money, I have no money."

Her father smiled. "We have the money Leon sends for the children tucked away for a rainy day. Honey, it's raining teardrops for your family right now. We've got to change it. The children belong together, and you and Leon have a responsibility to love and nourish them. Call him and tell him you're coming. Get a motel room until you find a place to live. It isn't right that the family should be split up. Like I told you before, just tuck him into bed when he comes home. You belong together as a family."

Clare Jean's father meant well.
"Yes, father. I know we can't go on this way. I'll leave for Edison Cove tomorrow," said Clare Jean.

The phone rang later that day. It was Leon. "I found us a place, honey. Come home soon. Bring the kids with you. I've rented an older 4-bedroom home with a study where we can set up a desk and computer. I miss you, honey. I haven't drank in 3 weeks. Do you want to speak to Sadie? Sam's outside playing. Mom's taking a nap."

"Yes, Leon, let me speak to Sadie," Clare Jean answered happily.

"I'll put her on."

"Hello, Mama, this is Sadie. I miss you Mama. Daddy found us a house. Wait until you see it. It's got a big oak tree in the back yard and rose bushes. You always liked rose bushes. I love you Mama.

We'll live near Grandma, mom. She said she'd help you with taking care of us. We're going to be happy! Come quick. I'll put daddy on now."

After a pause, Leon got back on. "Hello, Clare Jean? When will you be here? Never mind, I'll come and get you. I'll be there tomorrow. Can you be ready?" he asked.

"Yes, Leon," Clare Jean said hesitantly. "Yes, I can be ready."

"Alright then. Until tomorrow. Bye, Love."

He hung up with Clare Jean still holding onto the phone in happy disbelief.

So they tried it again, in a different house. Clare Jean even got a part time job in an office. The kids were happy to have their parents back together. All seemed well. But then Leon went back to his old ways. Staying out late. The lipstick. The whole scene repeated.

One night when Leon didn't come home, Clare Jean decided to act. She put on her best outfit, called her neighbor, Fran, over to watch the children, and headed for Leon's stomping grounds, the "Forget Me Not" bar on Eighth and Emerson.

When Clare Jean entered the dim, smoky bar, the jukebox was playing "Please Release Me." Great, Clare Jean thought, here I am trying to hang onto my man and the damn jukebox is playing "Please Release Me." Just my luck.

"Hello doll," some intoxicated unfortunate said as he staggered over to Clare Jean.

Clare Jean thought quickly. "Sorry," she said, "You're not my type, Superman. Get lost!"

The drunk slunk away to the bar and sat down on a bar stool in disbelief. "I'll be damned. That bitch has spunk," he said aloud.

The bartender scowled. "Can it Oscar, or you can leave." Oscar canned it.

Clare Jean looked around, almost missing her husband sitting in a booth back near the restrooms. He was sitting with a woman. Leon spotted Clare Jean. His female friend spotted her, too, as Leon announced, "Here comes my wife. Happy days!"

"Yeah, Leon. Happy days," the woman said.

A new song came on the jukebox. You could hear the songstress singing, "One of these days, these boots are going to walk all over you." Except for the jukebox, the bar had gone completely quiet. The patrons turned on their stools to watch the fireworks about to happen.

Clare Jean looked directly into Leon's eyes and said, "They're playing my song. Who's your friend? Do you care to introduce me? No. Don't bother. Let me guess. Could it be Cindy sitting here shamelessly with my husband, a married man with a family? Or are you from the Salvation Army trying to save my husband's soul? I'll clue you in - it's too late. Go to hell, Leon. I had to see for myself. I'm going home to pack up your clothes in a nice neat pile on the front porch. I'll see you in court, Prince Charming." Clare Jean's inner being felt the pain of betrayal.

"Now, Clare Jean," Leon said, trying to appease her.

"I'm out of here." Clare Jean turned on her heels and walked out. As she let the door close behind her, the song ended and there was a low murmur in the bar. Then the voice of Cindy rose up. She was shouting angrily.

The next day was Saturday. The children happily played throughout the house unaware of the emotional state of their parents with their marriage on the rocks. Clare Jean busied herself in the kitchen cooking a roast and baking pumpkin pies. Leon was still sleeping on the couch. Outwardly everything looked normal, but a dark cloud hung over Clare Jean. She was miserable and undecided about what to do about her marriage. She decided to wait this one out. If I do nothing, maybe fate will intervene and mend my broken marriage, she thought. Hope is all I've got left. What little love I feel now for Leon could be put in a thimble. I found out the truth last night - the cold, hard truth. My husband is again seeing another woman. I'm not going to blame myself this time.

"It's in God's hands now. I've no longer got the strength to solve this on my own this time" she said aloud.

"What's in God's hands, Mother?" Little Jenna asked.

"Whether you get a cookie or not. Have you been a good girl?" Clare Jean answered lovingly.

"Yes, Mama," said little Jenna.

"Then, get yourself a cookie out of the cookie jar. Better yet, get a plastic bowl and take enough for all of your sisters and brothers."

"Wow, Mama! Okay. I love you, mother!"

Soon afterward, Leon woke up and came into the kitchen for a cup of coffee. He slowly poured it. Clare Jean held her breath, for time stood still for her. Out of the silence, Leon spoke up. "Clare Jean," he warned, "never come looking for me in the bars again or I'll leave you. You upset my friend."

"Friend or lover, Leon?" Clare Jean shot back, glaring at him angrily.

Leon shrugged his shoulders. "Oh, the hell with it," he said, and walked out of the room with his cup of coffee.

Clare Jean was too angry to cry. When he walked out of the

kitchen, the previous night came back to her, and she relived the whole scene.

"Yes, Leon, to hell with it," she uttered, slamming a hot pan onto the table. "I made a mistake and baked a cake," she said, and then broke out in hysterical laughter.

Leon came running in to the kitchen, frightened for her. "Clare Jean, are you alright?" he asked. She continued her hysterical laughter.

Leon called 911.

She was taken to General Hospital. Clare Jean had suffered a nervous breakdown.

Fran took care of the children. Clare Jean's work had called. Fran told Clare Jean's boss that she was sick in the hospital and wouldn't be coming into work for a while. Her boss told Fran that Clare Jean should take as much time off as she needed. Her job would be saved for her.

Clare Jean came home after several weeks. Even though she was out of the hospital, the end of the world had come to her. She no longer hoped. She no longer cared. She just sat depressed, staring at nothing in her home, singing church hymns, thinking, "Only God can save me now."

She went through the motions of living, but felt nothing except for a dull ache in her heart, not even able to shed a tear.

Life went on.

The first week back to her office job was rough for Clare Jean. But then she met Andy, and her mind started to heal.

She realized a happiness in Andy's good-natured ways towards her. He would bring coffee often to her desk to tempt her to take time for a small coffee break to talk with him.

Those were happy moments.

Then one day the happiness started to dwindle.

"Clare Jean," Andy said during their coffee break, "my wife has been sick a lot lately, and I finally talked her into going to the doctor. The doctor did some tests and it turns out she has cancer. The doctor said it is in the advanced stages and she doesn't have long to live. I am beside myself with guilt. I have not done right by my wife, and I'm no better than your husband, for I have been tempted to stray from her side more than once. Did you hear me, Clare Jean? You don't seem to be listening," Andy said, with sadness and despair in his voice.

"I'm sorry, Andy. I feel so bad for you and your wife. I was speechless for a moment and at a loss for words on what to tell you. Maybe she'll beat the cancer." Clare Jean wanted to believe in a miracle for Andy's wife.

"No, Clare Jean. She is going to die. I'm such a bastard. I even thought about having an affair with you. What will I do without her? I love her. My God, without her, I'm nothing," Andy said.

"Andy, get a hold of yourself. You have time left to be with her until the end. Be good to her and love her. I am your friend. If there is anything I can do to make it easier for you, let me know and I will do it. Trust in God. He'll see you through this."

"Thank you, Clare Jean, but I believe God has forgotten about Alice and me." Andy was now in tears.

"No, Andy, He hasn't forgotten you. Trust in Him to see you through this. I'm here for you, Andy. I'm here for you," Clare Jean repeated.

"Thank you, Clare Jean. We better get back to work. I'm going home early today, so I won't see you until tomorrow. See you then, Clare Jean. See you then."

"Yes, Andy, See you then," Clare Jean said, smiling at him kindly as he left.

The days passed by differently now for Clare Jean. Although she couldn't hope for herself, she hoped for Andy and his wife, Alice. The moments she had with Andy at work were precious to her. As she herself thought about life and death, she seriously started contemplating divorce, especially when Leon informed her he needed to get away and was taking a vacation to Florida alone.

As she was shopping for groceries one day Clare Jean met up with Dan, who worked with Leon. After friendly hellos he said, "Your husband told everybody he's taking his wife to Florida. I'm surprised. You didn't want to go with him? I got a card from him from Florida just yesterday."

"No, Dan, I didn't go. He didn't invite me," Clare Jean said sadly.

"I'm sorry, Clare Jean, I didn't know," Dan said before moving on.

That did it. "Leon took his wife to Florida and it wasn't me," Clare Jean told the judge when she went to get her divorce. The divorce was granted. She was now a free woman legally, but not emotionally.

Life went on.

Andy was missing a lot of work. When he was there he was full of guilt and remorse for not being a better husband to Alice. She died not long after Clare Jean's divorce.

Both Andy and Clare Jean grieved together. They comforted one another. "I was a rotten husband," Andy told her. "I could have done so much more for her. My eyes wandered several times during our marriage. I never carried the casual affairs far enough to threaten our marriage. I don't know if Alice knew if I was playing around occasionally or not. She never said anything. And now it's too late to make it up to her. She's dead! Clare Jean. My wife is dead. I loved her. What am I going to do? And the bills. I'll never get them paid. I'm free now to offer you marriage, but I'm a pauper. The bills, Clare Jean. My God, how am I ever going to pay them?" Andy worried aloud to her.

"Don't punish yourself, Andy. She's gone. Nothing in God's name is going to bring her back. You've got to be strong for the children," Clare Jean sadly advised.

"She suffered so towards the last. I let her down---I let her die!" Andy said.

"No, Andy. You weren't responsible for her death. She was sick. You did the best you could. God called her home. It was her time to go. Your children need you. Love your children and comfort them. The bills will get paid. I have a little extra money set aside. I'll help you. Leon pays good support money. I can give you money every now and then to see you through the rough spots."

Hope came into Andy's heart. "Maybe we can marry then, Clare Jean. Are you willing?" he asked.

"Oh, yes, Andy! I'll marry you as soon as you're ready. I have a big home. There's plenty of room for the kids. Together we'll make it."

Andy and Clare Jean were married shortly afterward.

Leon was furious. He called his lawyer and took her to court when he learned she was using part of her support money to pay Andy's bills. He told the judge, "My ex-wife's taking money for what I send to support my family and paying that loser of a new husband of hers back bills. I won't have it, judge. That money is for the children."

"Are the children well taken care of?" the judge asked.

"Why, yes sir, she's a wonderful mother," was Leon's answer.

"Then if the children are properly provided for, you don't have a case. Case dismissed!" Down went the gavel. "Next?" said the judge.

Leon knew he had lost everything. His home, his wife, and now, most of all, his paycheck.

"It's time I quit drinking," he said to himself but he didn't listen to his own advice. He stopped at the nearest bar after the judge's decision and got drunk. He stayed all day. Then all evening. Finally, he was the last one to leave after last call. He wandered into the cold night and realized that he had nowhere else to go to. He had hell, he decided. As he staggered into a lonely motel room, he repeated aloud to himself, "And then there was hell."

It was late on a Friday night. Clare Jean sat on the couch in her new home. It was warm. No cockroaches. Real curtains on the windows. A soft glow from a new lamp, and the kids asleep in their rooms, safe and sound and together again as a family. Andy had just gone off to bed. Clare Jean decided to call her friend Martha. They hadn't spoken in ages!

Clare Jean dialed the phone. "Hello? Martha? Yes, it's Clare Jean! How have you been? That's great! Oh, a lot has changed. Have you got a few minutes? I'll tell you all about it. So where was I? Oh yeah. I remember now. I was pregnant, and my mom was coming. And the roaches were everywhere...."